THE VAMPIRE

THE VAMPIRE

By John Polidori
Adapted by Les Martin
Text illustrations by Paul Van Munching
Cover illustration by Paul Jennis

STEP-UP CLASSIC CHILLERS™
RANDOM HOUSE 🏠 NEW YORK

Library of Congress Cataloging-in-Publication Data:
Martin, Les, 1934–   . The vampire / by John Polidori ; adapted by
Les Martin.   p.   cm.—(Step-up classic chillers) SUMMARY: A young
Englishman traveling on the Continent with the mysterious Lord
Ruthven comes to realize that his companion is an evil and murderous
vampire.   ISBN: 0-394-83844-0 (pbk.); 0-394-93844-5 (lib. bdg.)
[1. Vampires—Fiction. 2. Horror stories] I. Polidori, John William,
1795–1821. Vampyre. II. Title. III. Series.
PZ7.M36353Vam   1989   [Fic]—dc19   88-34078

Manufactured in the United States of America   1 2 3 4 5 6 7 8 9 10

Chapter 1

The year was 1825. England was enjoying a beautiful autumn. I was eighteen years old. And I felt like the luckiest young man in the world.

I was just out of school. My guardian gave me enough money to live as I wanted to in London. And I had been invited to one of Lady Mercer's famous parties.

The most interesting people in London came to Lady Mercer's parties. I was wide-eyed the moment I entered the crowded room. I saw politicians and poets. I saw society ladies and actresses. I saw the rich. The powerful. The beautiful.

Then I spotted a man across the room. And everyone else at the party faded from my sight.

He was tall and slender. But he gave the impression of strength. He was dressed entirely in black. The same color as his hair. It was a sharp contrast to the color of his face.

That face reminded me of a marble statue. A statue of the Greek god Apollo. It was as handsome as that statue. And it was as pale.

It was the palest face I had ever seen on a human being. The palest face on anyone alive, at least. For I had seen that pallor once before. I had seen it on the faces of my dead parents just before they were buried. I was only ten at the time.

Then I saw the tall stranger's eyes. And the thought that he was anything like a corpse vanished.

There was nothing dead about those eyes. Even from across the room, lightning seemed to flash from them when they met mine. I felt blinded, until I forced my eyes away.

As I did, I saw a tight smile appear briefly on the man's lips. It was like a ripple on a sea. A sea as smooth as glass.

"Who is that man?" I asked a pretty girl. She had started to chat with me.

Her name was Caroline Standish. She had come to London to hunt for a husband. She clearly looked on me as a possible catch. But she clearly looked at the man across the room very differently.

Her eyes grew large. She bit her lip. She was like a child gazing at sweets in a candy store window.

"His name is Lord Ruthven," she said. Her eyes stayed fixed on him. It was as if she was half hypnotized by the sight of him.

"Tell me about him," I said.

"There's little I can tell you," she

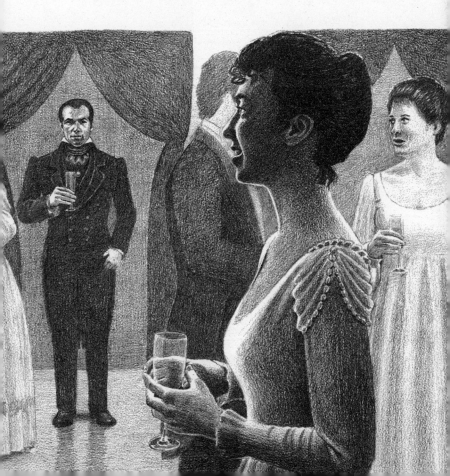

answered. "Lord Ruthven is the most mysterious man in London. Doubtless that is why Lady Mercer invited him here. She likes guests who get attention. Wherever Ruthven goes, eyes turn and tongues wag."

"And what do those wagging tongues say?" I asked.

"So many different things," she answered. "He is ages older than he looks. He is much younger. He is rich. He is poor. He is kind. He is cruel. He adores women. He hates them.

"But no one knows for sure what he is really like," she added. "He lets no one close enough to him to find out."

"And would you like to be the one to find out?" I asked. I could not resist teasing her.

"I would not dare to," she said. "I know not why, but just the sight of him makes me shiver."

"You may get a chance to see him better now," I said. "Look! He is coming toward us."

Her eyes grew even wider. Her creamy skin had a strawberry blush.

"I must go," she said nervously. "Mamma would be very angry if she saw me talking to him."

I barely noticed her as she ran off. I had eyes only for Lord Ruthven.

He came closer and closer. I might as well have been alone in the room with him. Then he reached me. And we stood face to face.

Chapter 2

He wasted no time in introducing himself. "Ruthven," he said.

"Aubrey," I answered. My voice was as cool as his.

I did not want him to notice that a shiver had run through me when he spoke. Perhaps the same shiver that Caroline Standish had described.

"You interest me, Aubrey," he said.

"Really?" I said. "Why?"

"People who stare at me always interest me," he said.

"Then you must be interested in everyone in this room," I said.

Again a ghost of a smile appeared on Ruthven's lips. "Well said, Aubrey. I can see that you may be worthy of my interest. Tell me about yourself. Begin with your family."

His tone of voice demanded that I obey him. Normally I would have been annoyed. His question was like a command. But my resistance melted when I looked into his eyes.

I must here describe those eyes. Before I met Ruthven, I had seen such eyes. Certain kinds of cats had them. They were eyes as gray as storm clouds. But they had a burning yellow fire in their centers.

The power of that yellow fire had struck me from across the room. It was a thousand times stronger close up. It burned into my brain.

"I have little family to tell you about," I said. "There is only my sister, Annabelle. Our parents died years ago. Fortunately, they left enough money for us. Our guardian could send us to excellent schools."

"Your sister, is she older or younger than you?" Ruthven asked.

"Younger, by a year," I told him.

Ruthven's eyes burned brighter. "And what does she look like, this sister of yours?"

I pulled a small round silver case from my pocket. I carried it with me always. In it was a portrait of Annabelle.

Ruthven studied it. "You and she look very much alike."

"People often say we could be twins," I agreed.

"I knew there was a reason for wanting to know you, Aubrey," Ruthven said. "I have a sixth sense about such matters. Your sister is most beautiful. I would like to meet her. You must arrange it."

By now I was completely in the power of his burning gaze. Still, I had to say, "Sorry. There's no way I can do it. Annabelle's boarding school frowns upon male visitors. Even I can see her only briefly."

"When does she get out of school?" Ruthven asked.

"In the spring," I said.

"I suppose I must wait until then," Ruthven said. His shrug seemed to snap his hold on me. For a moment, I felt unsteady, off-balance. It was as if I had woken from a dream.

Ruthven went on in his cool voice. It was as if nothing strange had happened. "Clearly I cannot meet your sister now. Then I'll have to make do with you alone, Aubrey."

"But what could you find to do with me?" I had to ask.

"Fill my empty hours with an amusing task," Ruthven said. "I am a man who has done and seen everything. You are the opposite. I have a great deal to teach. You have a great deal to learn. A perfect match, don't you think?"

Here was a dazzling man of the world! He wanted to be my guide to the pleasures of that world. How could I say no?

But how much better for myself and others if I had!

Chapter 3

Ruthven kept his promise to teach me how to live as a gentleman should. He took me to boxing matches and horse races. He let me sit in his box in the theater. He introduced me to drinking and gambling. He polished my manners. He sent me to the finest tailors. But still he was not satisfied.

"You must come abroad with me," he declared. "Europe is alive. London is dead. After dark the

streets are as empty as a graveyard."

"With good reason," I said. "People fear to go out at night."

I was referring to a recent series of mysterious deaths after dark. Bodies of young women had been found drained of blood. There were puncture marks on their necks. Those marks seemed made by serpent's fangs. But of course there were no snakes loose in London.

"Whatever the reason, life here has grown stale," Ruthven answered. "I hunger for change. Join me. I promise you a feast of travel and adventure."

I hesitated. Then Ruthven added in a teasing tone, "Besides, Miss Caroline Standish and her mamma seem determined to trap you into marriage. Escape before they succeed.

"Don't lose your freedom," he added. "You have barely begun to enjoy it. You have youth, good looks, and wealth. They can win you so many tender young girls."

"You flatter me," I said.

"No, I envy you," Ruthven said. "I have no such luck. Mothers keep their precious daughters away from me. I have resisted wedlock too long. They no longer hope to catch me. But you, Aubrey, have no such problem."

Should I have guessed the truth then and there? Should I have suspected why Ruthven wanted me with him on his travels? But how could I? The truth was so monstrous!

I suspected nothing. A week later I set sail with Ruthven for Italy. It was only in Rome that the truth began to dawn on me.

The first hint came shortly after our arrival in the Italian capital. I received a letter. It was from my guardian.

My guardian had heard disturbing stories about Lord Ruthven. A number of young ladies who had spent time with him had vanished. They were never seen again. It was as if the earth had swallowed them whole.

There was no proof against Lord Ruthven. But my guardian had put two and two together. He urged me to break with Ruthven at once.

I crumpled up that letter and

threw it away. And I did not even bother to ask Ruthven about those stories.

I was sure I knew who had made them up and why. Mothers made them up to scare their daughters. Those mothers wanted to keep their daughters from falling in love when there was no chance of marriage. It was the price that Ruthven had to pay for his independence. It only made me admire him more.

I was filled with admiration for Ruthven those first days in Rome. He knew everyone and everything. He gave me a guided tour of the city. He made its long history come alive. He described it vividly. It was as if he had been there a thousand years ago.

Ruthven gave me a guided tour of
Roman society as well. He was wel-
come in the mansions and palaces of
the oldest families. It seemed they

had known him for a long, long time.

I had every reason to admire him. I was grateful to him as well. And my gratitude grew even stronger. One night he took me to a party. A party I will never forget.

Chapter 4

The party was given in Ruthven's honor by the Countess Calvino. She was a woman long past youth. She wore thick makeup and dazzling jewels. But they could not hide her age. Strangely, most of the women invited to her party were quite young.

I asked Ruthven about this. He answered, "The Countess wanted you to have dancing partners your own age. Take advantage of her generosity, or she will be insulted."

I needed no urging. I danced with

one girl after another. Ruthven and
the Countess watched me approv-
ingly. Then I danced with Sophia
D'Angelo.

Sophia had dark hair and a heart-
shaped face. Her innocent eyes and
sweet smile made my heart pound.
She was as light as a feather in my
arms. The moment the dance ended,

I asked her for the next.

"I would like to," she said in lightly accented English. "But I cannot dance twice in a row with the same man. My mother is very strict."

Sophia pointed to a stern looking woman. She was keeping an eye on us.

"Then we can just talk," I said.

"I hope so," she said. "But it is up to my mother to decide."

Sophia's mother asked me about my age, education, family, and income. She looked me up and down. Finally she nodded. She left Sophia and me to talk by ourselves.

I do not remember what we talked about. I only remember that her voice was like lilting music. The evening passed like a dream. When it ended, I knew that I had to see Sophia again.

I said as much to Ruthven as we returned to our hotel.

"I congratulate you on your choice. And on your conquest," Ruthven said.

"Hardly a conquest," I protested. "We've barely met."

"Take my word," Ruthven said. "I saw the way she looked at you. She will do whatever you want."

He smiled. "Sheltered girls. No wonder their mothers protect them so carefully. They have no defenses."

Then Ruthven smiled at me. There was a touch of warmth in his tight-lipped smile.

"I must congratulate myself on my

choice as well," he said. "I was right to think you were worth my time and trouble. You, my dear Aubrey, are rewarding my faith in you."

Still I did not suspect the truth. I thought Ruthven was being kind. But the next day I learned the cruel truth.

Chapter 5

"I told you so," Ruthven said the next morning.

"So you did," I agreed. "By now I should know to believe you always."

I had received an invitation to Sophia's for dinner. That day I went to a barber Ruthven recommended. I had Ruthven help me choose the proper dinner clothes. And that evening I went to Sophia's, full of confidence.

The maid brought me into the reception room. And then the storm broke!

The mother's eyes were blazing. "How dare you come here? What is your game? Sophia's father is out searching for her. If he were here, he would kill you on the spot."

"I don't understand," I said.

"Perhaps you will understand this note. I found it in her room," she said.

Dearest Sophia,
  I must see you alone. Meet me at the Spanish Steps at sunset. If you do not, you will lose me forever.
          With all my love,
          Aubrey
P.S. Burn this.

"But the little innocent! She was too

sentimental to burn it," the mother cried. "What have you done with my baby?"

I did not waste time answering. I recognized the expensive notepaper. I had been with Ruthven when he bought it at a London shop.

"Come," I said. "We must hurry."

I gave a cabby a gold piece to lash his horse to a gallop. We raced to the hotel. I went up the stairs two at a time. Sophia's mother was panting right behind me. I ran full tilt against Ruthven's locked door and smashed it open.

Ruthven and Sophia stood facing each other. Her eyes were glazed. Her arms hung limp at her sides. His hands were on her shoulders.

In seconds, a weeping Sophia was dragged out of the room by her mother. And I faced Ruthven.

Ruthven was as calm as I was angry. Before I could demand an explanation, he gave me one.

"I was concerned about you," he said. "I did not want you to fall into the clutches of the wrong woman. I decided to test her. You can see how quickly she went off with me. I have saved you! That girl surely would

have betrayed you."

"You expect me to believe that?" I said scornfully.

Ruthven raised his eyebrows. "You do not?"

"Now I believe the letter I received from my guardian," I answered. And I told Ruthven what it had said.

"Lies," Ruthven said. "Common people cannot stand anyone who dares to be different."

"At first I thought so," I said. "But now I see why you wanted me on this trip. To be a lure for your prey."

"Come now, Aubrey," said Ruthven. "You need only look into my eyes. You will see I have no evil designs."

But by now I knew too well the

power of Ruthven's gaze. Those gray eyes! They could make even a girl like Sophia lose her will to resist him.

Without another word, I turned and left the room. I packed my things. Then I departed from the hotel. I vowed to leave Ruthven and all memory of him far, far behind.

Chapter 6

A ship from Italy took me to Greece. There I found a beautiful and unspoiled country. And I found a beautiful and unspoiled girl as well.

At school, I had dreamed of being an artist. Greece inspired me to start painting again.

I tried to capture the clear light in my paintings. The wonderful colors of field and forest, mountain and sea. And the treasures of the past. Ruins from the golden age of Greece.

Ianthe was my guide. Her father was the local innkeeper.

She knew the countryside as only a native could. Ianthe showed me wonders of nature no tourist would spot. She led me to ruins no looters had found.

And she warned me of dangers. As an Englishman, I found them hard to believe.

"Beware of bandits," she said. "The Turks still rule here. But they are weak. The land is lawless."

"Don't worry," I told her. "I have a pair of pistols. They were made by the finest gunsmith in London."

She sighed. Her hazel eyes filled with concern. But she saw it was useless to argue. I was too young to recognize risk. I was too eager to impress her with my courage.

"At least believe this," she said. "There is a danger your pistols cannot guard against. Please. Do not go into the forest here at night."

"What waits there?" I said with a smile. "Bears? Wolves?"

"Far worse," she said. "Have you ever heard of—vampires?"

I continued to smile. "Vampires? You mean evil creatures who suck the blood from humans?"

"You do know of them," she said with relief. "You will be careful."

"I know of them as I know of goblins and ghosts," I said. "Only children believe in them."

"Maybe in England," she said. "But here it is different. *We* know they exist—to our sorrow."

I continued to make light of her worries. "What do they look like? Do they have horns? Tails? Long sharp teeth?"

Ianthe shook her head. "Only one person has seen one and lived. A young woman was saved by the sun.

It rose as the vampire was about to feast on her. She saw a tall man. He was as handsome as one of the old statues."

"A devil with the face of a god," I said. A shiver ran through me.

"What's wrong?" Ianthe asked.

"Nothing. A silly thought," I answered quickly. "Let's talk of more pleasant matters. Let's talk about how much I love you."

"You say you love me. Then promise not to go into the forest at night," Ianthe begged.

I tried to calm her. "Come now. How many victims has this creature claimed lately?"

"None since the attack on the woman fifty years ago," Ianthe said.

"Then this vampire must have died

of starvation. Or old age," I joked.

"A vampire does not age," Ianthe answered. "And it has many hunting grounds. It returns to a place only when fear has faded. That might take fifty years. But it waits—and returns."

Ianthe put her hand on my arm. "Please. Promise not to go into the forest. Promise, if only for my sake."

I shrugged. "All right, I promise. For your sake."

I meant to keep that promise. I swear I did. I tell that to myself again and again. But nothing I say can change what happened. Or take away the guilt I still feel.

Chapter 7

There was a wedding party in the village. Ianthe had to help her father in the inn. So I went out in the countryside alone.

I found two white marble columns. They were standing under a brilliant blue sky. I set about painting a watercolor of the striking scene. Time passed. The shadows grew longer. Then I realized that night was approaching.

I quickly packed my paints and

folded my easel. I was far from the village, and I did not want to lose my way in the dark. But the sun was setting by the time I reached the forest.

Cutting through the forest would save an hour. I did not hesitate. I plunged into the woods.

I soon saw my mistake. Outside the forest, it was still twilight. Inside it was pitch dark.

But I did not turn back. I moved straight ahead, feeling my way. Soon I would be at the inn. I could already see Ianthe's delight when I showed her my painting.

Then I heard a rustling sound and a chilling chuckle. I felt a sharp chop on the back of my neck. Then— nothingness.

Everything was still black when I

came to. I felt ropes binding my arms
and legs. A gag was in my mouth.

I heard a loud peal of thunder. A
flash of lightning showed me where
I was. I was on the dirt floor of a
hut.

I saw another light. The flickering
light of a torch. It lighted a face and
form as beautiful as an angel. Ianthe.

"Thank the good Lord! I am in

time," she said.

With the gag in my mouth, I could only grunt a muffled warning. A dark form had leapt from the shadows. With blinding speed it ripped her torch away.

Again there was darkness. Again a chilling chuckle. Then Ianthe screamed. Her cry of terror was snuffed out as swiftly as her torch.

It was followed by an even more horrifying sound. A slurping noise. The same noise as when a starving person attacks a bowl of soup!

After that, silence. Then more thunder. Then rain drumming on the hut's roof. And my heart pounding in the darkness.

At last the storm died. I heard voices coming nearer. Light flooded the hut. Three men with torches streamed in through the open doorway.

My gag was removed. "Stand aside," I said. "I have to see."

The men from the village did not

move. They blocked my view of Ianthe.

"Best you not look," one of the men advised.

"Untie me," I commanded.

He slowly obeyed. I heard the men talking.

"We warned Ianthe."

"She would not listen."

"She knew the risk."

"She was so worried about that Englishman."

"We should have come with her."

"We should not have waited so long to look for her."

"We were too slow. Too late."

"No use for this now," said the largest of the three men. He threw down a wooden stake. One end had a sharp point. It was as sharp as a spear.

By now I was freed. I stood up on trembling legs. I pushed through the wall of men. I looked down at Ianthe. And I fainted dead away.

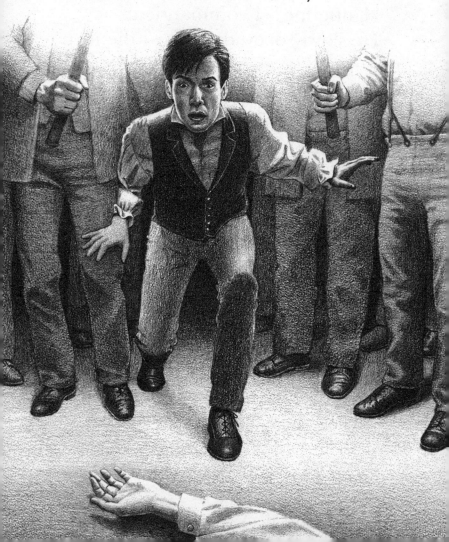

Chapter 8

I seemed to be asleep and dreaming. But it was no ordinary dream. All I saw was Ianthe's face. Her eyes were frozen open in terror. Her skin was chalk white.

Finally that death mask faded. A face with the same bloodless pallor took its place. Ruthven was looking down at me.

"You've come to at last," he said. "I feared you might not make it."

I realized I was lying in bed in my

room at the inn. I shrank from Ruthven's smiling gaze.

"You fiend," I gasped. "You succeeded in using me as a lure after all. You tied me down so that Ianthe would come looking for me. You sprang at her like a tiger on a lamb."

Ruthven did not blink. "My poor fellow. Do not excite yourself," he said. "You have been lying at death's door for eight days. You are still weak. Your mind is playing tricks on you."

"My mind has never been clearer," I said. "I now know who you are. *What* you are."

Ruthven spoke gently, as if to a child. "What am I then, Aubrey?"

I spat the words out. *"A vampire."*

Ruthven shook his head sadly.

"You have been in Greece too long," he said. "You have begun to think like a native."

"Don't try to pretend," I said. "You followed me here from Rome to regain your hold on me. You did not want to waste the time you invested in me. Then you discovered that Ianthe was in love with me. And you seized your chance."

"Nonsense," said Ruthven. "I wanted to patch up that foolish fight we had in Rome over that silly girl. What *was* her name again? Sandra? Serafina?"

"Sophia," I said coldly.

"Ah, yes, Sophia," Ruthven responded calmly. "A pretty little thing. But not worth our friendship. I followed you here to clear the matter up. Then I found you lying unconscious with a high fever.

"The innkeeper said something about a vampire," Ruthven continued. "His daughter was killed. Poor man. He refuses to admit that bandits did the dirty work.

"These villagers!" Ruthven said in disgust. "They would rather believe in forces they cannot control. It's lucky I arrived to nurse you back to health with modern medicines. They would have let you die. They would have said it was the work of the devil. Or God's will."

I could only say, "You expect me to believe that?"

Ruthven shrugged. "Ask the innkeeper. Or ask anyone else you care to."

"I'll do just that," I declared.

But when I did, I learned that Ruthven was telling the truth. The villagers said he had cared for me day and night. They swore he had worked a miracle. He had brought me back from the brink of death.

About Ianthe, they would say nothing. To them I was a foreigner. I was to be kept out of their private affairs. Only Ianthe had spoken to me with complete openness. The same way she had opened her heart for me. And now Ianthe was gone.

Nothing remained for me here but painful memories. Ruthven suggested that we leave as soon as I was strong enough. I agreed. Together we would explore the rest of Greece. Beyond that lay Albania and Turkey. Finally we planned to reach the fabled city of Constantinople.

But fate had other plans.

Chapter 9

We were riding fine black stallions through the mountains of northern Greece. Two other horses carried our baggage. A local guide rode in front of us on the twisting trail.

Ruthven was telling me about Constantinople. "A splendid city. It may be the capital of a dying empire. But it is full of life. Money can buy anything there. Families will sell their own daughters for—"

Suddenly our guide spurred his horse. He galloped away.

"What the—?" I exclaimed.

"Quick, get down!" Ruthven said. He brought his horse to a halt. Swiftly he slipped to the ground.

I did the same. I was just in time.

A rifle cracked. A bullet whizzed over my horse's empty saddle.

"Follow me," Ruthven ordered. He raced to a nearby boulder. We crouched behind it, drawing our pistols from our belts.

"Bandits," said Ruthven. "Our guide sold us out. Constantinople is not the only place where money can buy anything."

I cocked my pistol. "At least we'll make them pay dearly for—"

At that moment, Ruthven gave me a powerful shove. I went sprawling. He hurled himself on top of me. Just then a shot rang out. His body was lying over mine. I felt it jerk sharply.

"Drop your pistol, Englishman," said a heavily accented voice. "Stand up. Keep your hands in the air."

"Do as he says," Ruthven groaned as he rolled off me.

I stood up. A bearded bandit with a smoking rifle came out of the bushes behind us. I looked down. Ruthven lay on the ground. A bright

red stain was spreading on his white shirt.

"Your friend, he save your life," the bandit said. "But how he know I am going to shoot? I do not know. He must have the second sight."

I knelt beside Ruthven. I bent my head near his mouth to catch his words.

"This is twice now I have saved your life," he gasped. "In return you must promise me two things."

"Of course. Anything," I said.

"First, do not let the bandits bury me. I have a horror of lying under the earth. Have them carry me to a lonely place. A place open to the sky. Then leave me there."

"But you may not die," I said.

He ignored my feeble protest. He went on. "And back in England, do not reveal my death. Say nothing of what has happened in Europe. I want my name at least to remain alive. Free of scandal or suspicion."

"I may not get back to England alive," I said.

"You will," Ruthven said. "The bandits will ransom you when they learn you are rich. Now give me your solemn oath that you will do what I ask."

"I swear on my honor," I said.

"I do not believe in honor," Ruthven replied.

"I swear on all that is holy," I said.

"I do not believe in anything holy," Ruthven said.

"Then what shall I swear on?" I asked.

Ruthven's lips curved in a thin smile. "Swear on your blood."

"I swear on my blood," I said.

"Break your vow, and your blood is mine," Ruthven said. His voice rose in a last burst of life.

Then, still smiling, he shuddered. And slumped into death's final rest.

That smile! It mocked death as it

had mocked life. Gently, I lowered Ruthven's eyelids over his sightless eyes.

Only later did I realize what he was smiling at. By then, it was too late.

Chapter 10

Ruthven had vanished!

The bandits had laid his corpse on a cliff overlooking a deep ravine. They were willing to humor my request. I had told them that my guardian would pay them well for my release.

So when the money arrived, I was free. I went to say good-bye to Ruthven's remains. Not a trace of them remained.

"What have you done with his body?" I asked the bandit chief.

He shrugged and stroked his long mustache. "Me?" he said. "Nothing. But we are not the only ones in the mountains. Others must have found him there. They took his fine black suit and leather boots. Then they probably threw his naked body into the ravine. You have seen the last of your friend, Englishman."

Well, at least I had kept my word to Ruthven, I thought. And I would continue to do so when I returned to England. Not a word about his fate would pass my lips.

My promise seemed easy to keep. I traveled from Greece to Italy and then to France. At last I crossed the Channel to England. The closer I came to home, the more unreal Ruthven began to seem.

Even under gray June clouds, London looked wonderful. I met my sister, Annabelle, at the home of our guardian. She was even more lovely than I remembered. She seemed lit by a special joy.

"How happy you look," I said. "Is it so good to be out of school at last?"

"It's more than that," she said. "It's seeing you safe and sound, dear brother."

Then she paused. A blush came to her cheeks. "And there's something else as well."

"What is that?" I asked.

She turned toward our guardian. "Shall I tell him?" she asked.

"I don't see why not," the white-haired gentleman said. He beamed his approval.

"I have met the most perfect man in the world. We are going to be married," Annabelle said.

"Delighted to hear it," I told her. "Who is the lucky fellow?"

"The Earl of Marsden," she said.

"Marsden?" I said. "I don't believe I know him."

"It's a new name for him," my sister explained. "He inherited the title, when a distant relative died.

She was about to go on when my guardian interrupted. "We will let you see him for yourself. He is due to arrive here soon."

He exchanged a smile with my sister.

"Yes," she said. "We will let it be a surprise."

"At least tell me how you met him," I said.

"He paid us a visit," said my guardian. "It was shortly after we learned you had been kidnapped in Greece."

"He was worried about your safety," my sister said. Her eyes shone with love for her husband-to-be.

"He was such a help in freeing you," my guardian said. "He took care of everything. I think that is what truly won your sister's heart."

"Then I have even more to thank him for," I told my sister. "Though his making you so happy is enough to win my deepest gratitude."

"How happy he will be to hear you say that," my sister said. "As happy as I am to hear it."

At that moment, the butler entered the drawing room. "The Earl of Marsden has arrived," he announced.

"I'll bring him in to meet you," my sister exclaimed. She ran lightly out of the room.

A minute later she was back, holding the arm of her beloved.

He smiled when he saw me. That

thin smile I knew only too well.

"So good to see you again, Aubrey," Ruthven said.

Chapter 11

I opened my eyes and saw a room full of sunlight. I was lying in bed. For a moment I thought all that had happened was a bad dream.

The bedroom door swung open. My guardian entered. He smiled with relief when he saw me sitting up in bed.

"Thank God," he said. "You're better at last."

"Where am I?" I asked.

"In the upstairs guest room of my

home," my guardian answered.

"How long have I been here?" I asked.

"Two weeks," my guardian said. "Two very long weeks."

"Two weeks?" I said. "Impossible! It seems like just a moment ago that I found out—"

I stopped and shuddered at the memory.

"Please, don't excite yourself," my guardian warned. "It was foolish of us to have given you the news of your sister's engagement the moment you arrived. You could not stand all that excitement at once. Not after your terrible kidnapping. That is Lord Marsden's opinion. And I agree."

"Lord Marsden?" I said. Then I remembered. "You mean Ruthven."

"Lord Marsden now," my guardian said. "The good fellow was dreadfully upset when you collapsed. He sent his personal doctor to care for you. The doctor said you had brain fever. Such diseases are common in foreign lands."

My brain did feel feverish. But that was because it was working so hard. I had to think what to do now. I could not say that Ruthven had come back from the dead. That would land me in the hospital, if not the madhouse.

Then there was the promise Ruthven had tricked me into making. I had sworn not to reveal what I had learned about him in Europe.

I could only tell my guardian, "It was not brain fever. It was the shock

of seeing Annabelle with Ruthven.
You yourself wrote me what a terrible man he is."

"You mean, what a terrible man he
was," my guardian said. "Of course,
you do not know how he has
changed. And you were the one who
caused it. It was your break with him
in Rome. You made him see the error of his ways.

"He is a new man! He goes to
church. He helps the poor. Why else
would Annabelle fall in love with
him?" my guardian asked. "Why else
would I approve their match?"

My hands closed tightly under the
covers. But I kept my voice calm.
"When is the marriage to be?"

My guardian looked doubtful. "I
do not know if I should tell you. The

excitement might—"

"I feel perfectly fine. Completely recovered," I assured him. "I simply want to hear the good news."

My guardian was convinced. "I am sure the happy couple would want you to. They were so upset that you could not attend the ceremony."

"It's happened already?" I gasped.

To my relief, my guardian said, "No. It takes place this evening. A strange time for a wedding, I must say. But Marsden says it's a family tradition.

"It's supposed to bring good fortune and that sort of thing," he added. "Noble old families like his do have such ways. It sets them apart from ordinary folk."

"Where will the wedding be?" I

asked. I had already swung my legs over the side of the bed.

"Here in this house," my guardian said. "We hated to think of a wedding with you so ill. But it could not wait. Marsden has to go abroad. Italy. He and Annabelle leave tomorrow."

"I must see Annabelle alone right away," I said.

"But you are still weak," my guardian answered. "And she is busy getting ready. She can come up to see you after the wedding."

"I'm fine," I said in a strong voice. "And I want to see Annabelle now. It is my duty as her brother. Where is she?"

"In the second-floor guest room," my guardian said. He pulled out his gold watch. "But you hardly have time. The sun is about to set. The wedding is in less than an hour."

"I'll hurry," I said. I stood up and began to dress.

"At least take your medicine," my guardian said. "Marsden's doctor said you should have a dose every night."

He picked up a small brown bottle from my bedside table. "The nurse got a fresh bottle yesterday. It's still full!" he exclaimed. "She forgot to give it to you last night."

I opened the bottle and sniffed it. The smell was sweet and heavy. The smell of the drug called laudanum. It was made from opium. No wonder I had been in a daze so long.

I pretended to take a swallow. My guardian nodded and left.

I finished throwing on my clothes.

My room was on the third floor. I went down the flight of stairs two steps at a time. Without bothering to knock on my sister's door, I flung it open, praying Annabelle was there.

She was.

But she was not alone.

"Aubrey," Ruthven said. "What a surprise. How good of you to come to wish us a happy marriage."

Chapter 12

Ruthven had his arm around Annabelle's shoulders.

Annabelle said nothing. Her blank eyes told me she saw nothing as well.

"You fiend! Let her go!" I said.

"Surely it is up to her to decide," Ruthven replied. He cupped her chin in one hand. He turned her face up so that he could look into her eyes.

"You do want to be mine. Don't you, my dear?" he asked.

Her voice was faint. But her words were clear. "Yes, my love."

"You see?" Ruthven said with a shrug. "Your sister has made up her mind. And I do not think you have the power to change it."

"Annabelle! Listen to me!" I said.

My voice was almost a shout. But Annabelle gave no sign she had heard. She continued to look up at Ruthven like a helpless slave.

I could only beg for Ruthven's mercy. "Why her?" I said. "Surely you could find another victim to satisfy your horrible hunger."

"My hunger can never be satisfied for long," Ruthven said. For a moment a shadow passed over his pale face. "Sometimes I wish it *could* be. But I must forever find fresh blood. Or else suffer pain no human can imagine."

"I swore to you on my blood to keep silent about you," I said desperately. "Now I declare my oath broken. Take my blood instead of hers."

"If your blood could feed me, do you think you would still be alive?" Ruthven said. "Only the blood of an innocent girl can quiet my hunger. It is not your blood I need, but the blood of your blood.

"But she is so young," I pleaded.

Ruthven smiled his thin, mocking smile. "You don't want her to die? Then be happy. You can be sure your sister will never die."

"What do you mean?" I had to ask, though I feared the answer.

"Once and only once those of my race can choose a mate," Ruthven said. "For thousands of years, I have searched for a bride. A bride to bring warmth to the icy emptiness within me. I have looked for her in Europe and Africa, China and India.

"At Lady Mercer's party, I saw you," he said. "I sensed I was close to my heart's desire. When you showed me your sister's portrait, I knew my search was over."

"So that's why you took me under

your wing," I said.

"Of course. But you were useful in other ways as well," Ruthven said. "Sophia made my mouth water. And Ianthe was delicious."

Ruthven's voice grew stronger. His eyes locked with mine. "Now you can serve me again. It would make my pleasure complete. Do your duty as a brother. Come now. Give the bride away."

Chapter 13

Once again I felt myself pulled into the burning yellow centers of Ruthven's storm-gray eyes. But my love for my sister was pulling the other way. For a moment I felt as if I were being ripped in two. Then I broke free.

"Never!" I shouted. I flung myself at Ruthven.

He did not blink. He did not even try to escape my rush. He kept one arm around Annabelle. He used his free hand to catch me by the collar.

His strength was superhuman. I was as helpless as a baby in his grip. Easily he threw me crashing against a wall. A small table broke as I fell.

I lay stunned on the rug. I saw Ruthven through pinpoints of pain. He threw back his head and bared his teeth in laughter.

I say his teeth. But "teeth" is not the right word for what I saw for the first time. Ruthven's thin-lipped smile had never let me see into his mouth before. Now I saw a pair of fangs. They were sharply pointed and the color of dried blood.

"So you will not give the bride away," Ruthven said. "Then be our witness. Watch the kiss that will make her mine. And one of my kind forever."

His voice was an animal snarl of hunger. He turned his back on me to bury his face in my sister's neck.

I could not bear to watch. I turned my eyes away. Then, right before my eyes, I saw a splintered table leg. It had been torn from the table I had fallen against.

In a flash of memory, I saw again that sharp stake of wood. That stake the Greek villagers had carried to the hut. *They* had known what weapon to use against their age-old enemy. And now I knew as well.

"No!" I screamed.

Ruthven turned to face me. But he had no time to stop me. I rammed the point of wood deep into his heart.

I looked down at him. He lay motionless on the floor. Then my sister

was clinging to me.

"Aubrey, I had the most awful dream," she said. She looked down.

"*He* was in it. Who is he?"

"I'll answer all questions later," I promised. "But first we must deal with the matter at hand. Come downstairs with me. And agree with everything I say."

My explanation to our guardian was short and simple. "Ruthven revealed his true colors. He had no intention of marrying Annabelle. He broke into her room. He was about to take her away by force. I heard her scream and rushed to her aid. There was a struggle. Ruthven was killed."

"It was—terrible," my sister said. She played her part well. She sobbed

and buried her face in a handker-
chief.

"I was a fool to be taken in by that
man," our guardian said. "Thank
goodness you stopped him."

"We must tell the police," I said.

"Of course," said our guardian.
"Disturb nothing in the room before
the police arrive. But be sure of this.
No jury in England will find you
guilty of any crime."

The police arrived shortly. A ser-
vant led them upstairs.

But when they came down from
the room, they were angry.

"What kind of joke are you playing?" asked one policeman. "We
ought to bring charges against you."

"Joke?" I asked.

"Since when is a dead man a joke?"

my guardian demanded.

"Dead man?" the policeman said with disgust. "There is no dead man up there. That room is empty."

My sister turned to me. "What could have happened to him?" she asked.

I had promised to answer all her questions. But I could not answer that one.

I still cannot.

I do not know where Ruthven has gone. Even worse, I do not know where—and when—he will return.

I ask you, dear reader, do you?

Les Martin is a busy freelance author and adapter. He has a special skill for vividly re-creating the feel of whatever time and place he writes about. His stories are fast moving and exciting. The same dynamic qualities that make him an ace on the tennis courts. He lives in New York City.

Paul Van Munching illustrated two other Step-Up Classic Chillers: *King Kong* and *Dr. Jekyll and Mr. Hyde*. In addition to science fiction and fantasy books, his work can be found on record album covers and in magazines. His hobby is bicycle racing, and he enjoys repairing bikes as well. Mr. Van Munching lives in New York City.